The Kite & Caitlin

For my brother, Bob – *J.P.*

A Red Fox Book

Published by Random House Children's Books
20 Vauxhall Bridge Road, London SW1V 2SA

A division of The Random House Group Ltd
London Melbourne Sydney Auckland
Johannesburg and agencies throughout the world

1 3 5 7 9 10 8 6 4 2

First published in Great Britain in 1996
by The Bodley Head Children's Books

Red Fox edition 2000

Printed in Singapore by Tien Wah Press (PTE) Ltd

THE RANDOM HOUSE GROUP Limited Reg. No. 954009
www.randomhouse.co.uk

ISBN 0-09-956131-X

The Kite & Caitlin

Roger McGough

Illustrated by John Prater

RED FOX

The kite hadn't been out of the cupboard since the day it had arrived at Beech House.

On her fifth birthday, Octavia had unwrapped the parcel excitedly, pulled a face, and then passed on to the next gift.

And there were many.

Kites are not cuddly.
You cannot dress and
undress a kite.
You cannot wear one.

Kites do not miaow.
You can't curl up in
front of the fire
with a good kite.

The kite spent its first day behind the sofa, and the next fifteen years in the cupboard under the stairs.

Caitlin's mother came across it at a car-boot sale. "Just the thing
for Jack," she thought.
But Jack thought differently.

You can't play football with a kite.
You can't strum one.
You can't shoot aliens with
a kite.

A kite cannot be
plugged into the television.
A kite does not make an
unbearably loud noise.

The kite might have spent the next fifteen years in another cupboard
had it not been for Caitlin.
What Caitlin loved about the kite was its sadness.
She understood it.
The last two years had been spent in and out of hospital.
She was weak and could not walk.

"When you get better," said her mother, "you will be able to go up on a hill and fly the kite."

Mother and daughter smiled at each other. A sad smile. One that stayed in place too long to be true.

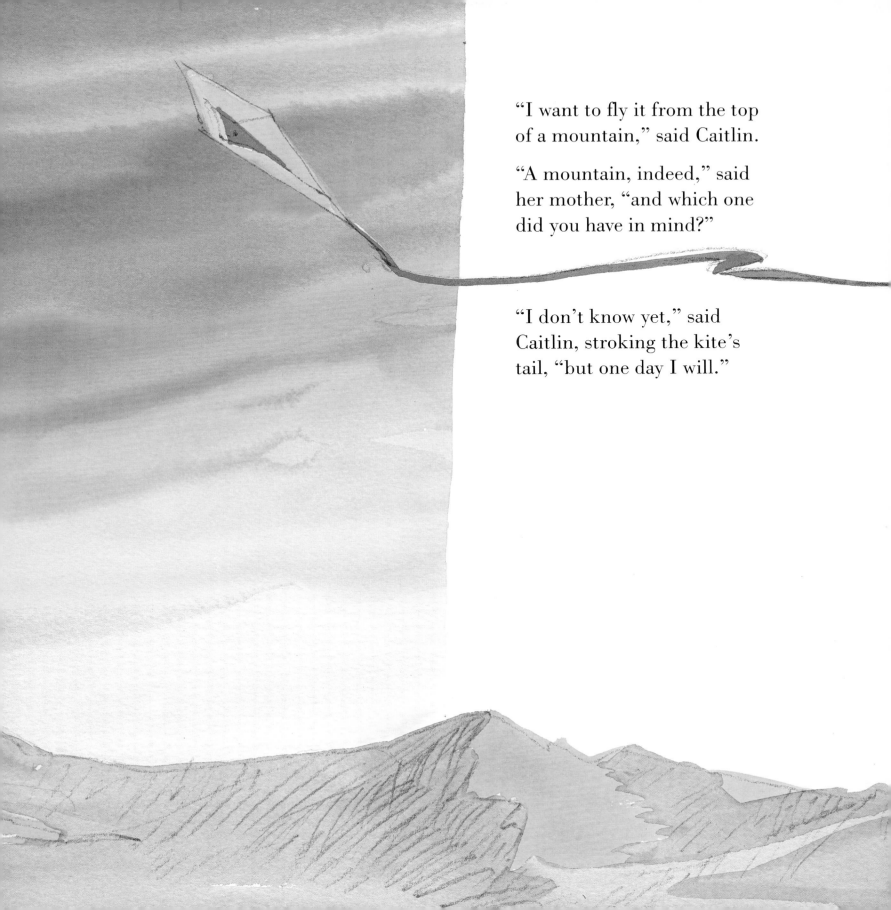

"I want to fly it from the top of a mountain," said Caitlin.

"A mountain, indeed," said her mother, "and which one did you have in mind?"

"I don't know yet," said Caitlin, stroking the kite's tail, "but one day I will."

Soon, Caitlin knew all there was to know about mountains (or rather, knew a little of all there was to know about mountains).

She learned that the highest mountain in Britain is Ben Nevis (1,342 metres).

That the highest mountain in Europe is Mont Blanc (4,807 metres).

That the highest mountain in Africa is Kilimanjaro (5,895 metres).

That the highest mountain in the U.S.A. is Mount McKinley (6,194 metres).

And that the highest mountain in the world is Mount Everest (8,848 metres).

8,848 metres

6,194 metres

5,895 metres

4,807 metres

1,342 metres

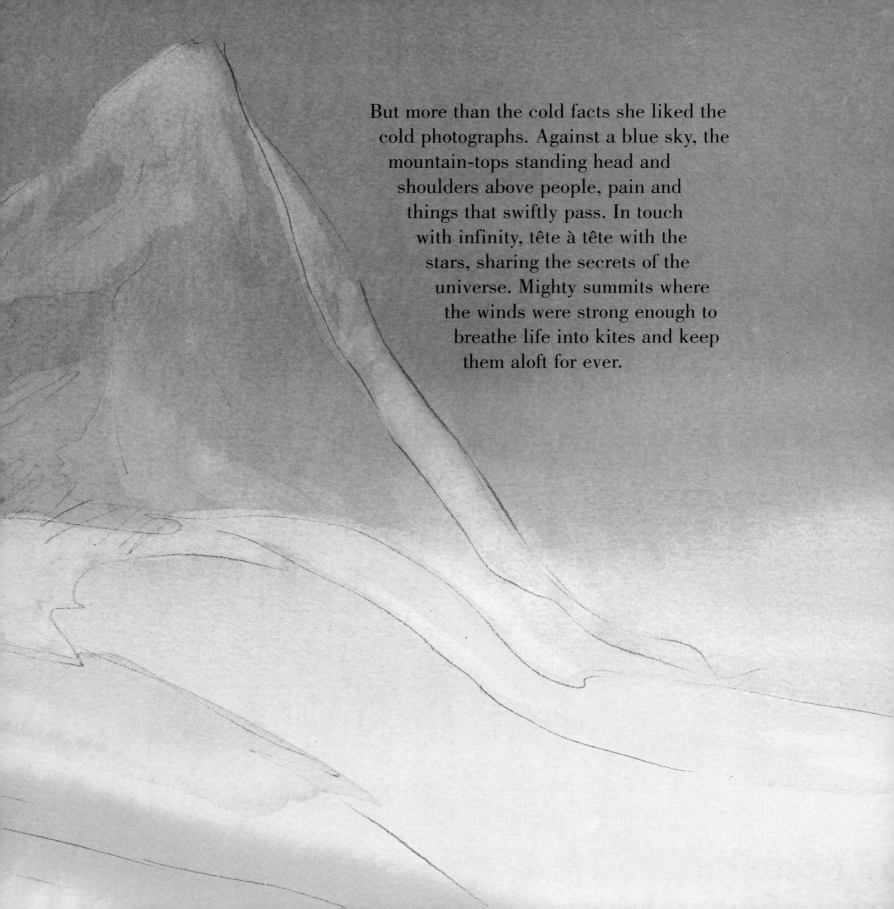

But more than the cold facts she liked the
cold photographs. Against a blue sky, the
mountain-tops standing head and
shoulders above people, pain and
things that swiftly pass. In touch
with infinity, tête à tête with the
stars, sharing the secrets of the
universe. Mighty summits where
the winds were strong enough to
breathe life into kites and keep
them aloft for ever.

It is Midsummer's Eve. So hot that nothing moves. In the garden, the leaves hang limp on the trees. The lawn wrinkles its brow trying hard to remember rain.

Only the cat is cool, curled up in a pool of moonlight.

In her bedroom, Caitlin lies on the bed limp as a leaf. Each breath a shadow of the one before, every heartbeat a fading echo.

High summer, and a leaf is about to fall from the tree.

"Hold tight," whispers the kite.

"Hold tight, and I will take you where the air is so fresh and pure, one breath is all you need."

And out of the window
and up into the windless sky
and over the parched fields
and the dry tongue of the river
and the cracked lips of the hills …

"We're going to a mountain,
aren't we?" asks Caitlin.
But the kite is silent now.

And up
and over
Loch Ness
(the monster
fast asleep in
the ice-box
of the deep).

"Is it Ben Nevis?"
asks Caitlin.

And up
and over
the Welsh Valleys
(the sheep on the
hillsides counting
each other before
dozing off).

"Is it Snowdon?"
asks Caitlin.

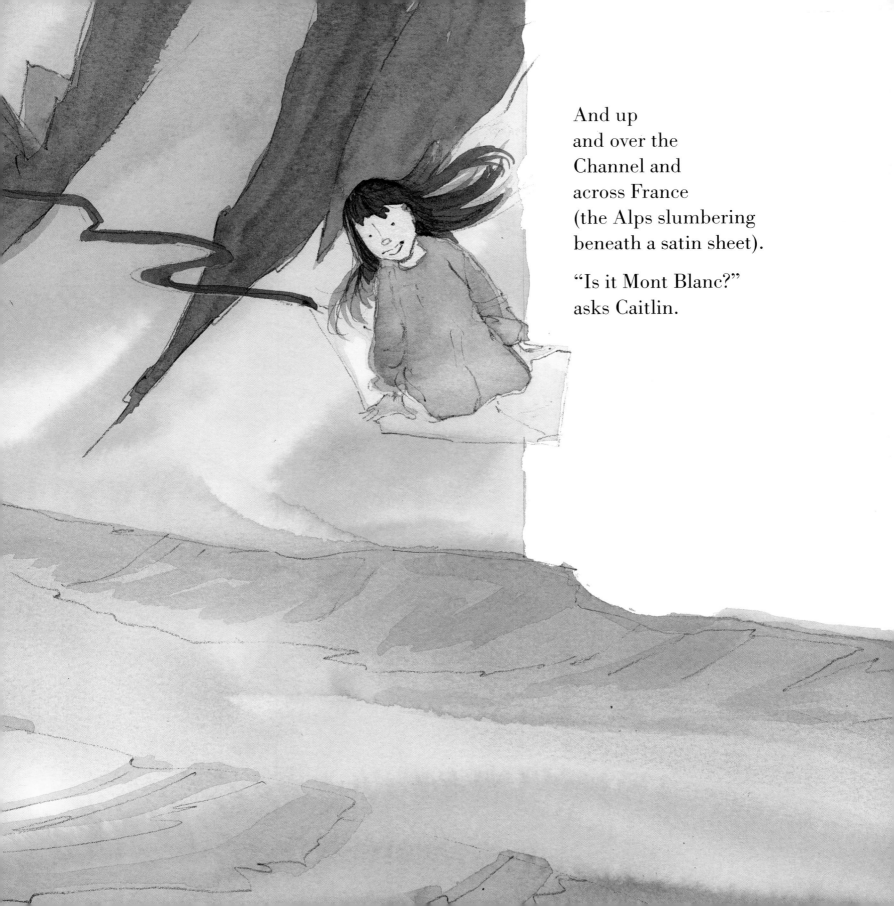

And up
and over the
Channel and
across France
(the Alps slumbering
beneath a satin sheet).

"Is it Mont Blanc?"
asks Caitlin.

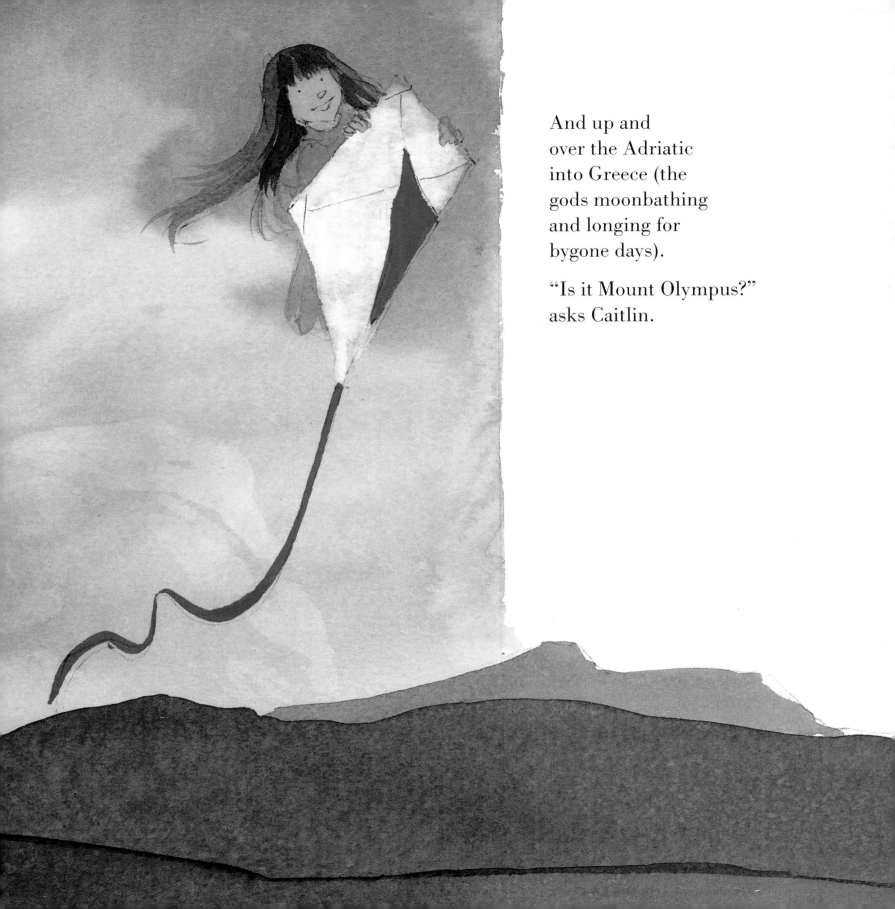

And up and
over the Adriatic
into Greece (the
gods moonbathing
and longing for
bygone days).

"Is it Mount Olympus?"
asks Caitlin.

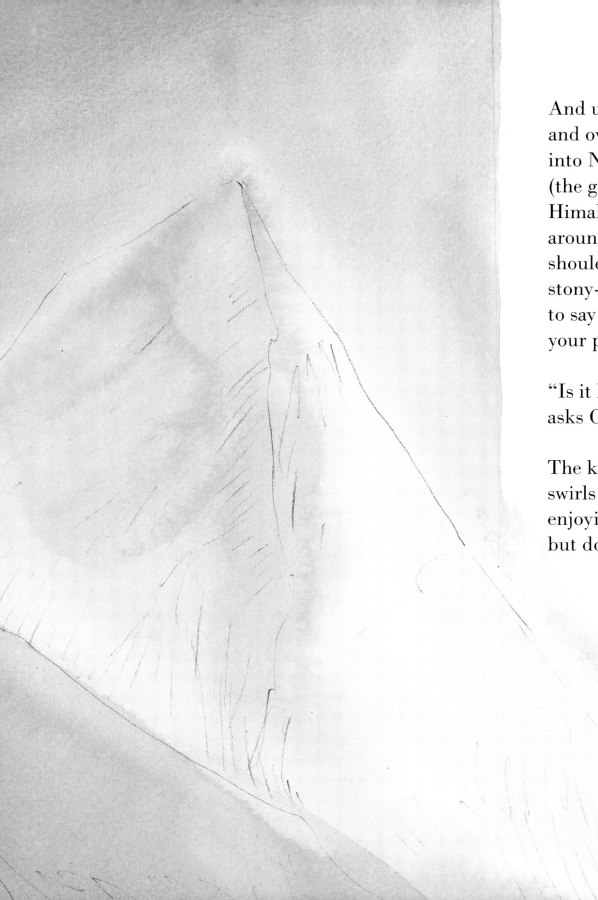

And up
and over India
into Nepal
(the giants of the
Himalayas, arms
around each other's
shoulders, glaring
stony-faced as if
to say: "Visit us at
your peril.")

"Is it Mount Everest?"
asks Caitlin.

The kite stoops and
swirls around the top,
enjoying the moment,
but doesn't stop.

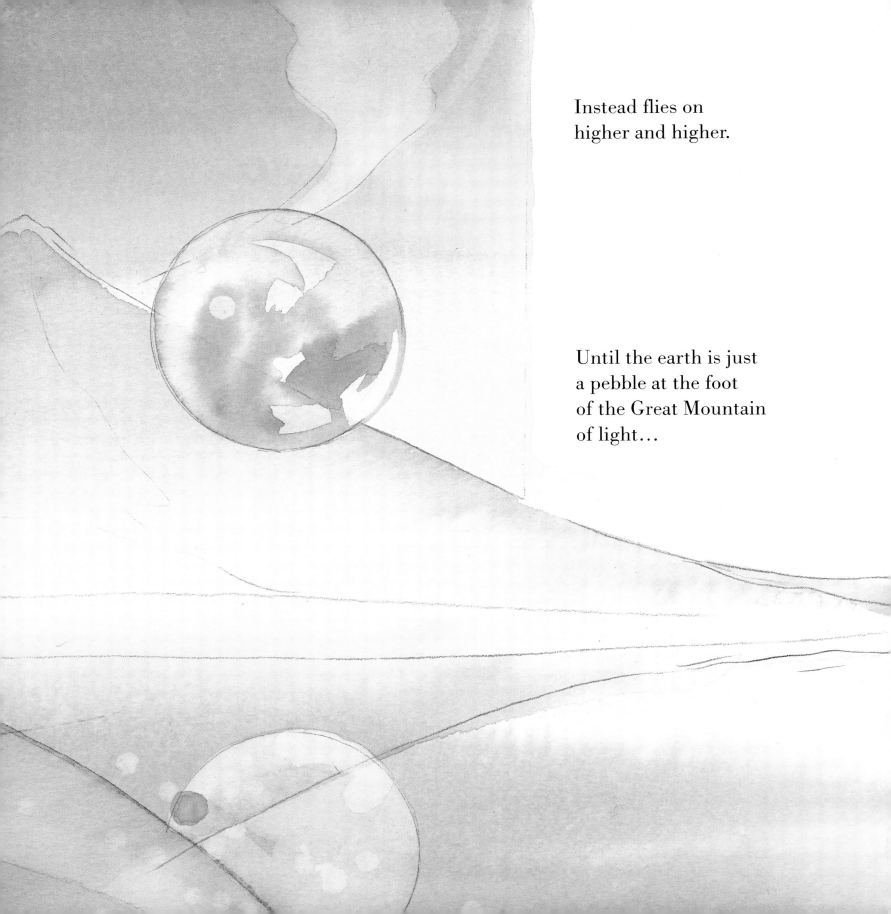

Instead flies on
higher and higher.

Until the earth is just
a pebble at the foot
of the Great Mountain
of light...

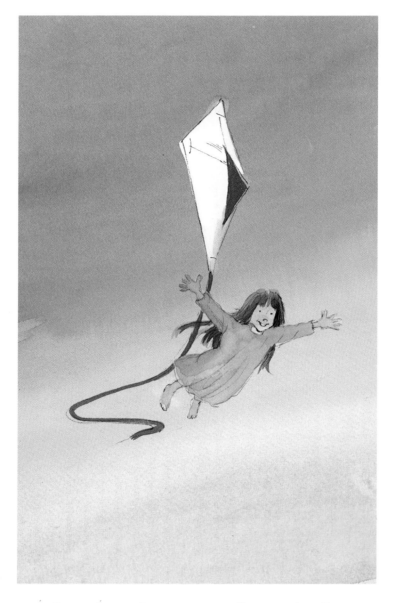

…where happiness ever after waits for
Caitlin and the kite.